D0719031

PRIDE AND PREJUDICE

& Emojis

1 3 5 7 9 10 8 6 4 2

Pop Press, an imprint of Ebury Publishing,
20 Vauxhall Bridge Road,
London SW1V 2SA

Pop Press is part of the Penguin Random House group of companies whose addresses can be found at global.penguinrandomhouse.com

First published by Pop Press in 2017

www.penguin.co.uk

A CIP catalogue record for this book is available from the British Library

ISBN 978 1 785 03737 5

Printed and bound in China by Toppan Leefung

PRIDE AND PREJUDICE

& Emojis

Cast of Characters

Elizabeth Bennet
Mr Darcy
Jane Bennet
Lydia Bennet
Mary Bennet
Kitty Bennet
Mr Bingley
Mr Bennet
Mrs Bennet
Mr Wickham
Mr Collins
Caroline Bingley
Mrs Hurst
Mr Hurst
Charlotte Lucas
Lady Catherine de Bourgh
Miss de Bourgh
Sir William Lucas
Maria Lucas
Georgiana Darcy
Mr Gardiner

Mrs Gardiner
Colonel Fitzwilliam
Colonel Forster
Mrs Forster
The housekeeper at Pemberley

List of Abodes

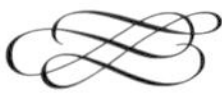

Longbourn
Pemberley
Netherfield Park
Rosings
Hunsford
Lucas Lodge
The Assembly Room
Meryton
London
Brighton
Derbyshire

Chapter 1

It is a truth universally acknowledged that a single man in possession of a good fortune must be in want of a wife.

'My dear Mr Bennet,' said his lady, 'have you heard that Netherfield Park is let? By a young man of large fortune. Four or five thousand a year!'

'Well I will not visit him,' answered her husband. 'But I will send a few lines to assure him of my hearty consent to his marrying whichever he chooses of the girls; though I must throw in a good word for Lizzy.'

'You take delight in vexing me…' replied his wife.

Chapter 1

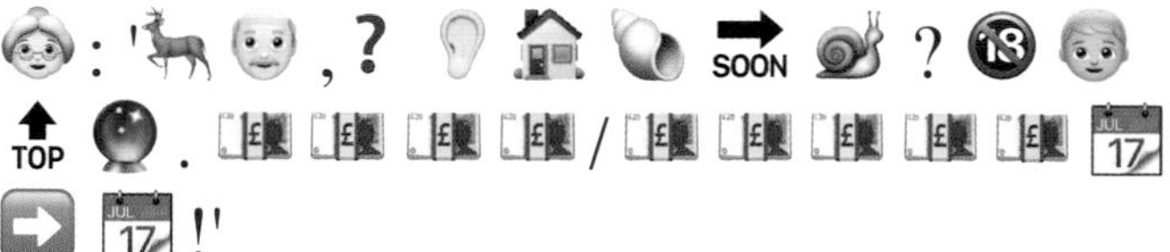

Chapter 2

'Don't keep coughing so, Kitty, for Heaven's sake! My poor nerves,' said Mrs Bennet. 'And I am sick of hearing of Mr Bingley, as we shall never meet him.'

'If I had known that this morning,' replied her husband, 'I should never have called on him.'

'You have called on him! What an excellent father you are!'

'Now Kitty, said he, 'I suppose you may cough as much as you wish…'

Chapter 2

Chapter 3

Mr Bingley attended the assembly with his two sisters and another young man, Mr Darcy, whom it was rumoured had £10 thousand a year.

Mr Bingley was widely admired, for his good looks and easy manners; Darcy was discovered to be the proudest, most disagreeable man in the world.

Elizabeth was diverted to hear herself thus described: 'She is tolerable but not handsome enough to tempt me.'

Chapter 3

💁‍♀️ 🤣 👂 💁‍♀️ ⬅️ 💬 :
🎩 : '💁‍♀️ 🟰 🆗 , 🚫 🔥 💅 ➡️ 😋 🎩 . '

Chapter 4

'He is just what a man ought to be,' said Jane, after they got home. 'Sensible, good-humoured, lively; and, with such perfect good breeding! And I imagine his sisters will be charming neighbours.'

Elizabeth was not convinced.

....

Back at Netherfield, Bingley stated that he had never met with such pleasant people or prettier girls in his life; Miss Bennet was pronounced an angel!

Mr Darcy acknowledged that she was pretty, but said she smiled too much.

Chapter 4

Chapter 5

Charlotte Lucas, a sensible, intelligent woman, about twenty-seven, was Elizabeth's intimate friend. She came to visit Longbourn the morning after the assembly.

Mrs Bennet said to her with civil self command, '*You* began the evening well, Charlotte. *You* were Mr Bingley's first choice.'

'Mr Bingley may have danced with me first,' said she, 'but I think he liked his second choice better.'

'Yes, he danced with Jane twice,' boasted Mrs Bennet.

After questioning from the others about Mr Darcy, Elizabeth promised never to dance with him.

Chapter 5

Chapter 6

Charlotte said to Elizabeth, at a party at Lucas Lodge, 'If Jane is too guarded with her affection, she may lose the opportunity of fixing Bingley. In nine cases out of ten, a women had better show more affection than she feels.'

'Perhaps. Why is Mr Darcy watching me?'

'My dear Miss Eliza,' said Sir Lucas, 'why are you not dancing? Mr Darcy, you must allow me to present this young lady to you.'

Mr Darcy, with grave propriety, requested to be allowed the honour of her hand. She declined.

Chapter 6

💁‍♀️: '🤷‍♀️. ⁉️ 🎩 👀 💁‍♀️ ? '

👴🏿: '🦌 💁‍♀️, ? 🚫 💃. 🎩, 🎟️ 👴🏿 2️⃣ 🎁 👇 🔞 🚺 ➡️ 🎩.'

🎩, ⚰️ 🙇, 🙏 🎟️ ✋. 🙅‍♀️.

Chapter 7

Jane received a letter, inviting her to Netherfield for dinner. 'You should go on horseback,' said her mother, 'because it looks likely to rain; and then you must stay all night.'

Jane wrote the next day, 'MY DEAR LIZZY – I find myself very unwell this morning, which, I suppose, is to be imputed to my getting wet through yesterday.'

Elizabeth walked to Netherfield, arriving with dirty ankles and a face glowing from the exercise. Miss Bingley looked disapproving, but invited her to stay.

Chapter 7

💁‍♀️ 🚶‍♀️ ➡️ 🏠, 💩 🔛 👢 ➕ 😊 ⬅️ 🏋️.
👸 🙄, 🍑 ✉️ 🎟️ 💁‍♀️ 🛏️ 🏠.

Chapter 8

The party were playing cards and asked Elizabeth, 'Will you join us at loo?' Suspecting them to be playing high, she declined.

'How is your sister Georgiana, Mr Darcy?' cried Miss Bingley. 'She is so accomplished! I think, for a woman to be accomplished, she must have an in-depth knowledge of music, singing, drawing, dancing, and the modern languages; and she must possess a certain something in her air and manner of walking, the tone of her voice, her address and expressions.'

Elizabeth was bemused.

Chapter 8

💁‍♀️😕.

Chapter 9

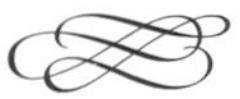

Mrs Bennet arrived to check on her daughter.
'She is a great deal too ill to be moved,' she told the party, 'but she has the sweetest temper!'

Elizabeth tried to prevent her mother from talking further and embarrassing herself, without much luck.

Lydia reminded Mr Bingley of his promise for a ball at Netherfield.
'You shall choose the day!' he responded.

Miss Bingley and Mrs Hurst had the pleasure of roundly abusing them all on their departure.

Chapter 9

Chapter 10

Mr Darcy was writing a letter to his sister, Georgiana, while Miss Bingley complimented him on his handwriting and the evenness of his lines.

'Will one of you ladies play the pianoforte?' he asked.

Miss Bingley moved with some alacrity to the instrument.

Elizabeth felt Mr Darcy's eyes on her all evening. She thought to herself, *he must dislike me*.

Chapter 10

🎩: '👸🆚👸🆚💁‍♀️🎹?'

👸🏃‍♀️🎹.

💁‍♀️👀🎩🌅➡️🌌.
💁‍♀️💭: '🎩😠➡️💁‍♀️.'

Chapter 11

Miss Bingley could not distract Mr Darcy from his book, so invited Elizabeth to walk around the drawing room. He soon closed his book to watch them.

Elizabeth found occasion to laugh at him, and pick at his pride.

Darcy told her, 'My temper would perhaps be called resentful. My good opinion, once lost, is lost forever.'

He realised he might be in danger of falling for Elizabeth.

Chapter 11

Chapter 12

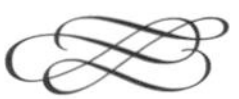

Jane's health improved dramatically, so the sisters desired to return to Longbourn.

On Elizabeth's final day at Netherfield, Mr Darcy did not speak to her, and was relieved at her departure. He didn't want to elevate her with the hope of influencing his felicity.

....

Elizabeth and Jane returned home, to a cold welcome from their mother, but pleasure from their father.

Chapter 12

Chapter 13

Mr Bennet said at breakfast one morning, 'A month ago I received a letter from my cousin, Mr Collins, who, when I am dead, may turn you all out of this house as soon as he pleases.'

He read the letter aloud, which spoke a lot of Lady Catherine de Bourgh, of his offering a olive branch to the family, and of coming to stay.

When Mr Collins arrived at Longbourn, he spent the whole evening complimenting Mrs Bennet on the house, the dinner, the wine, the furniture and the beauty of her daughters.

Chapter 13

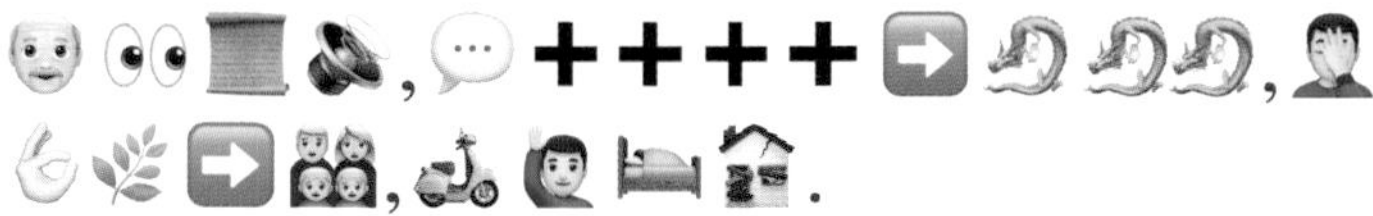

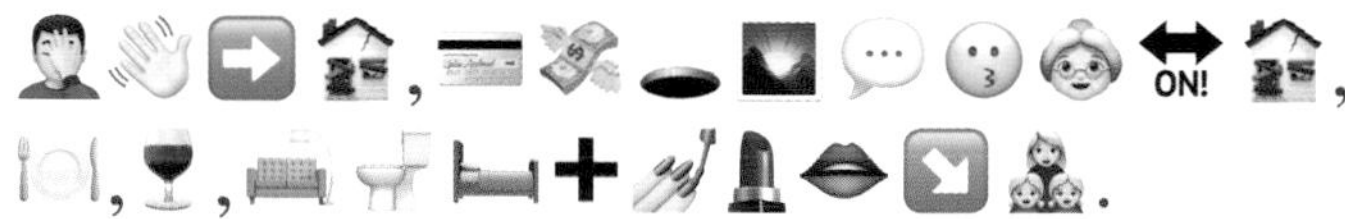

Chapter 14

Mr Collins talked on and on about the condescension of Lady Catherine de Bourgh, and her sickly daughter.

'I am happy to offer those little delicate compliments which are acceptable to ladies,' said Mr Collins.

'You judge very properly,' said Mr Bennet.

Mr Collins read to them from a very serious book, but Lydia rudely interrupted him to talk about the officers.

Chapter 15

Having a good house and a very sufficient income, Mr Collins wanted to marry; and he meant to choose one of the daughters.

Jane was his first choice, but Mrs Bennet informed him that she might soon be engaged, so he changed to Elizabeth.

....

The whole party walked to Meryton, where they met a very attractive officer, Mr Wickham. While talking with him, Elizabeth heard the sound of horses; Darcy greeted them, but on seeing Mr Wickham, the countenance of both changed colour.

Chapter 15

Chapter 16

In Meryton, that evening, while the others played at cards, Mr Wickham sat beside Elizabeth; she very much enjoyed his conversation.

'Has Mr Darcy been in this neighbourhood long?' asked he. 'I have been connected with him since my infancy. The world is blinded by his fortune, but he has treated me ill. His father wanted me for the church, but when he died, his son did not honour his promise.'

'Shocking!' cried Elizabeth.

Mr Collins lost very badly at cards.

Chapter 16

Chapter 17

That night, Elizabeth repeated to Jane what Mr Wickham had told her. 'Oh dear,' said Jane, 'there must be a mistake and nobody has acted wrong at all.'

Mr Bingley came to Longbourn to deliver an invitation to the Netherfield Ball by hand.

'I hope to engage you, fair Elizabeth,' said Mr Collins, 'for the first two dances.'

Mr Collins's proposal was accepted with as good a grace as she could manage.

Chapter 17

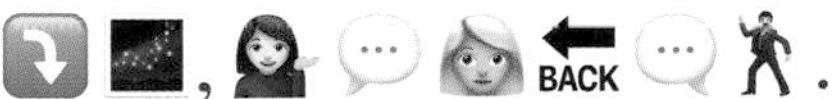

Chapter 18

At the Netherfield Ball, Elizabeth's first disappointment of the evening was that Mr Wickham was not there. Then began her catalogue of embarrassments:

~ Dancing with Mr Collins;

~ Awkward conversation while dancing with Mr Darcy, while attacking him for his evil treatment of Mr Wickham;

~ Miss Bingley being rude;

~ Mr Collins talking to Mr Darcy of Lady Catherine;

~ Her mother talking loudly about Jane marrying Mr Bingley;

~ Mary singing;

~ Her father stopping Mary singing.

Chapter 18

- 👯👯➕🤦‍♂️
- 😬💬💬↔️👯➕🎩, 👊😈👈➡️🕺

- 👸🟰🖕😝
- 🤦‍♂️💬🎩⤵️🐉
- 👵💬📣⤵️👰⛪🥂🙋‍♂️

- 👩‍💻🎤🎶
- 👴✋🚫👩‍💻🎤🎶

Chapter 19

In the course of the morning, Mr Collins requested an audience with Elizabeth. 'Before I am run away with my feelings,' said Mr Collins, 'I should first state my reasons for wanting to marry: first, I think it right for a clergyman to marry; second, I believe it will add to my happiness; third, it was the opinion of Lady Catherine de Bourgh.'

Elizabeth replied, 'I am very sensible of the honour of your proposals, but it is impossible for me to do otherwise than to decline them.'

'I believe it is usual for elegant females to reject a first proposal, but I shall hope to lead you to the altar ere long.'

Chapter 19

Chapter 20

On hearing what had Elizabeth had said, her mother reassured Mr Collins: 'Oh Lizzy is a headstrong girl! I will speak to her father.'

'Oh! Mr Bennet,' said she, 'you are wanted upstairs immediately; we are all in an uproar. Please make Lizzy marry Mr Collins!'

Mrs Bennet led Elizabeth to her father, who told her, 'An unhappy alternative is before you, Elizabeth. From this day on, you must be a stranger to one of your parents. Your mother will never see you again if you do not marry Mr Collins, and I will never see you again if you do.'

Chapter 20

Chapter 21

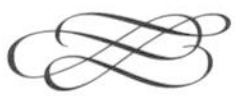

On the morrow, Mrs Bennet was in ill-humour and ill-health. Mr Collins went to Lucas Lodge to lick his wounds.

....

The sisters walked into Meryton, where they met with Mr Wickham. Elizabeth asked him why he did not attend the ball. 'I found,' said he, 'as the time drew near, that I couldn't bear to be at a party with Mr Darcy for so many hours together.'

....

That evening Jane received a letter from Caroline. It said that the whole party had left Netherfield to go to town – and without any intention of coming back again.

Chapter 21

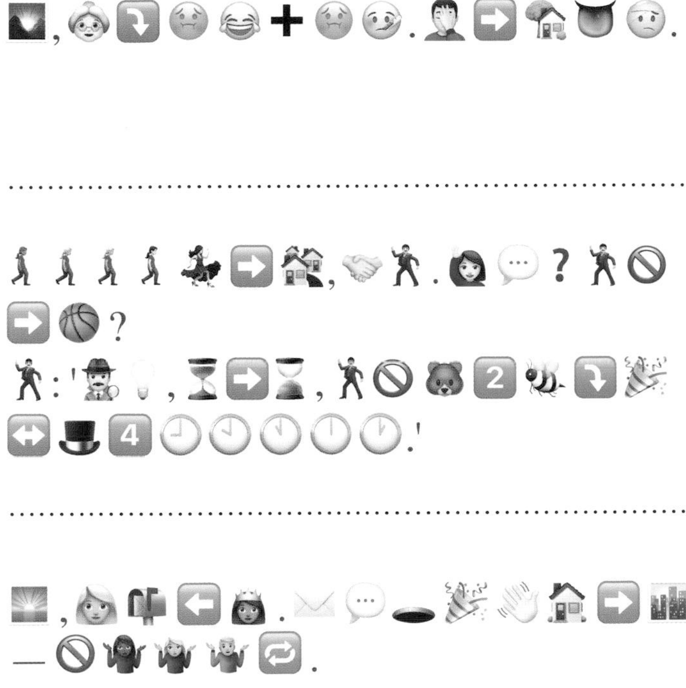

Chapter 22

'Engaged to Mr Collins!' cried Elizabeth. 'My dear Charlotte – unthinkable!'

Earlier that morning, Mr Collins had gone to Lucas Lodge to propose to Charlotte; she accepted him. Without thinking highly either of men or matrimony, marriage had always been her aim; it was the only option for well-educated women of small fortune.

Charlotte did not enjoy telling Elizabeth, who could not understand it.

Mr Collins left Longbourn, with a promise that he would return, if Lady Catherine would approve.

Chapter 22

Chapter 23

'Good Lord!' exclaimed Mrs Bennet. 'Sir William, how can you tell such a story? Do not you know that Mr Collins wants to marry Lizzy?'

Lizzy had to step in to help Sir Lucas convince her mother of the truth of it.

When he had left, Mrs Bennet was inconsolable. She could not stand that one day she might be turned out of Longbourn, to make way for Charlotte Lucas.

'My dear,' said her husband, 'do not give way to such gloomy thoughts. Let us hope for better: I may be the survivor!'

Chapter 23

Chapter 24

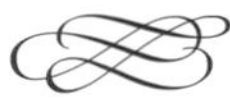

Jane received another letter from Miss Bingley, stating that the party would not return to Netherfield that winter, and contained repeated expression wishes for her brother's marriage to Miss Darcy.

'He will live in my memory as the best man of my acquaintance,' Jane told Elizabeth. 'I have nothing to reproach him with.'

'My dear Jane!' exclaimed Elizabeth, 'you are too good. Your sweetness is really angelic.'

Chapter 24

Chapter 25

Mrs Bennet's brother and his wife came to stay. Mr Gardiner was a greatly superior to his sister, as well by nature as education. His wife was an amiable, intelligent, elegant woman.

Mrs Gardiner spoke to Elizabeth of Jane's sad tale, and suggested, 'Do you think a change of scene would be good for Jane? She could return with us to London?' Elizabeth agreed.

Mrs Bennet arranged many parties during their stay, at which Mr Wickham was a regular face.

Chapter 25

Chapter 26

Before she left, Mrs Gardiner warned Elizabeth to be on her guard with Mr Wickham. Elizabeth promised to act wisely, but soon discovered his affection had shifted to a Miss King, who had inherited £10,000.

Charlotte married Mr Collins, but before leaving for Husford, she extracted a promise from Elizabeth to visit soon.

Jane wrote that she had not seen Mr Bingley in town, and his sister had evidently decided to drop the friendship with Jane.

Chapter 26

Chapter 27

In the spring, Elizabeth left Longbourn for Hunsford with Sir William and his daughter Maria; both amiable but empty-headed.

On the way, they stopped in London for a night to stay with Mr and Mrs Gardiner, and to see Jane. In a tete-a-tete, her aunt said that Jane was unhappy, but bearing it well. She also invited Lizzy on a tour of the lakes in the summer.

'Oh, my dear, dear aunt,' she cried, 'what delight! What are men to rocks and mountains?'

Chapter 27

Chapter 28

Arriving at the Hunsford parsonage, Mr Collins invited the party to admire every room, piece of furniture and view from his garden.

Charlotte bore it well. She confided to Elizabeth, 'I encourage him to be in the garden as much as possible.'

Mr Collins also had an announcement: 'I'm delighted to tell you that you have the good fortune of an invitation to dine at Rosings this evening!'

Chapter 28

Chapter 29

Lady Catherine was a tall, large woman, with strongly-marked features. Her daughter was pale and sickly.

Lady Catherine gave a great deal of advice to Charlotte on domestic matters, and instructed her as to the care of her cows and her poultry.

She asked all about Elizabeth's sisters and their education, whether she played and sang, or if she drew.

Elizabeth was forthright with her opinions, which surprised Lady Catherine a great deal.

Chapter 29

Chapter 30

The entertainment of dining at Rosings was repeated twice a week, and Elizabeth passed most of her hours walking in the woods around Huntsford.

Elizabeth found out Mr Darcy was soon to come to Rosings, and was interested to see how he would act with Miss de Bourgh, who apparently he was destined to marry.

Soon after his arrival, Mr Darcy came to call on them at the parsonage, with a Colonel Fitzwilliam. She asked Mr Darcy, 'Did you never happen to see my sister back in London?'

He looked a little confused, and answered in the negative.

Chapter 30

Chapter 31

On Easter Day, the party was invited to Rosings. Colonel Fitzwilliam sat by Elizabeth, and found she had not been half so entertained at Rosings before. He invited her to play the pianoforte, and Darcy came over to watch.

'Do you mean to frighten me, Mr Darcy?' she asked. She told Colonel Fitzwilliam that when she had met Mr Darcy at a ball, he had danced only four dances, and barely spoken to anyone.

'I am ill-qualified to recommend myself to strangers.' She pointed out the folly of such a statement.

Chapter 31

Chapter 32

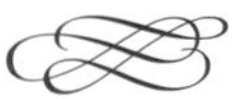

Elizabeth was alone at the parsonage, when Mr Darcy called. She enquired whether Mr Bingley would be likely to return to the neighbourhood, and he answered that he thought he would not.

He soon went away but he and Colonel Fitzwilliam called at the parsonage frequently in the coming days.

Mr Darcy was usually silent when he called but Charlotte wondered if he were in love with her friend. He certainly looked at her often.

Chapter 32

Chapter 33

On a walk in the woods, she encountered Colonel Fitzwilliam. They walked together, and the conversation led to Mr Bingley.

'Mr Darcy is uncommonly kind to Mr Bingley,' said Elizabeth drily, 'and takes a good deal of care of him.'

'Indeed,' he answered, 'Darcy congratulates himself on having saved Mr Bingley from a most imprudent marriage.'

Elizabeth's excess of emotion, from Colonel Fitzwilliam's communication, brought on a headache. She did not go to Rosings that evening.

Chapter 33

Chapter 34

Alone at the parsonage, Elizabeth was amazed when Mr Darcy arrived!

'My feelings will not be repressed,' he told her. 'You must allow me to tell you how ardently I admire and love you.'

He talked of the inferiority of her family and connections, and his struggle not to love her. She grew angry. 'Do you think that anything could tempt me to accept the man who has ruined the happiness of a most beloved sister? And I know of how you acted towards Mr Wickham.

'I had not known you a month before I knew that you were the last man on Earth whom I could ever marry.'

Chapter 34

Chapter 35

The next morning, Elizabeth went out for a walk, ill-suited for any other occupation. Mr Darcy found her, and gave her a letter, which sought to address the two offences she'd charged him with:

He acknowledged that he'd seen Mr Bingley to be very much in love with Jane, but believed she'd had no depth of feeling in return, so Mr Darcy had worked to separate them.

Then he told the story of Mr Wickham, who had resolved against the church, instead asking for pecuniary advantage. He wasted all his money, and when Mr Darcy would not help him one more time, he tried to elope with Miss Darcy.

Chapter 35

Chapter 36

As she read, Elizabeth hardly knew how to feel. His belief of her sister's insensibility she instantly resolved to be false; but, when she read his account of Mr Wickham, astonishment, apprehension, and even horror, oppressed her.

She had been blind, prejudiced, absurd. And then she began to understand what he had said about Jane: though her feelings were fervent, they were little displayed.

She returned to the parsonage to find that Mr Darcy and Colonel Fitzwilliam had called in her absence, to announce their departure.

Chapter 36

Chapter 37

Lady Catherine de Bourgh observed Elizabeth's low spirits, and assumed it was owing to her imminent departure from Hunsford.

'Write to your mother,' said she, 'and beg that you may stay a little longer. If you will stay another month complete, it will be in my power to take you to London. Young women should not travel alone, but always be properly guarded.'

'You are all kindness, but I believe we must depart a week hence.' And so they did.

Chapter 37

Chapter 38

After pressing Elizabeth to express her gratitude, Mr Collins bid them adieu.

As they departed, Maria commented, 'We have dined nine times at Rosings, besides drinking tea there twice! How much I shall have to tell!'

Elizabeth added privately, 'And how much I shall have to conceal!'

When they reached London, Elizabeth was pleased to see that Jane looked well, but Elizabeth had little opportunity of studying her spirits, amidst the various engagements. But Jane was to go home with her, and at Longbourn there would be leisure enough for observation.

Chapter 38

Chapter 39

Lydia and Kitty met the party on their journey back to Longbourn, with a lunch of cold meats. 'We mean to treat you all,' said Lydia, 'but you must lend us the money. I have bought this bonnet instead.'

Lydia had lots of news for them. 'The militia are going to be encamped in Brighton; I do so want papa to take us all there for the summer! Also, there is now no danger of Wickham's marrying Mary King!'

All the way home Lydia talked and laughed loudly, while Elizabeth tried not to listen to her.

Chapter 39

Chapter 40

Back at Longbourn, Elizabeth told Jane the story of Mr Darcy's proposal and letter.

Sisterly affection for Elizabeth lessened Jane's shock on hearing of Mr Darcy's love, but she was sorry for the unhappiness which her sister's refusal must have given him.

News of Mr Wickham touched her deeper – she would willingly have gone through the world without believing that so much wickedness existed in the whole race of mankind.

But the two sisters decided not to acquaint Meryton with the truth about him.

Chapter 40

Chapter 41

It was the last week of the regiment's stay in Meryton; the ladies in the neighbourhood were devastated. But then Lydia received an invitation from Mrs Forster to go to Brighton! Lydia was in ecstasy!

Elizabeth felt she had to warn her father of the dangers of not checking Lydia's exuberant spirits. He didn't listen.

Mr Wickham came to dine at Longbourn on his last evening in Meryton. Elizabeth talked of Hunsford and seeing Mr Darcy there, and she intimated that she knew the truth of his past. He looked worried.

Chapter 41

Chapter 42

A fortnight before Elizabeth was to tour the Lakes, a letter arrived from her aunt. Her uncle's business in London prevented a long trip, so she would have to content herself with Derbyshire.

At first she was excessively disappointed but it was not in her nature to be unhappy long. At last, they set off.

When the party stayed in an inn near Pemberley, her aunt expressed a wish to see the place again.

On discovering Mr Darcy was not at home for the summer, Lizzy agreed to go.

Chapter 42

Chapter 43

Elizabeth was delighted with Pemberley. 'Of this place,' thought she, 'I might have been mistress!'

The housekeeper took them round, informing them that her master was due in the morning with a party of friends, and talked at length of what a kind and generous master he was.

But when they had gone outside, who should Elizabeth meet but the master himself! Their eyes met, and their cheeks were overspread with the deepest blush. But he was all politeness, asking to meet her aunt and uncle, and inviting Mr Gardiner back to fish.

Elizabeth was amazed!

Chapter 43

Chapter 44

On the very morning of their arrival at Pemberley, Miss Darcy and Mr Bingley called on Elizabeth – with Mr Darcy.

Georgiana was not proud, as Mr Wickham had said, but rather was painfully shy; Mr Bingley was as good-humoured as before.

Mr Darcy invited them all to dinner at Pemberley.

After they left, Elizabeth spent a long time hoping to work out her feelings towards Mr Darcy. She certainly no longer hated him.

Chapter 44

Chapter 45

Mr Gardiner left soon after breakfast to go fishing with Mr Darcy, so the ladies followed to call on Miss Bingley, Mrs Hurst and an embarrassed Miss Darcy. When Mr Darcy arrived, Miss Bingley mentioned Wickham, which was painful to many.

When they left, Miss Bingley said to Darcy, 'How very ill Miss Eliza Bennet looked this morning – so coarse! I believe you thought she was rather pretty, at one time?'

'Yes,' replied Darcy, 'but that was only when I first saw her, for it is many months since I have considered her as one of the handsomest women of my acquaintance.'

Chapter 45

Chapter 46

Elizabeth received two letters from Jane. The first said that Lydia was gone off to Scotland with Wickham! The family hoped they would soon be married.

The second letter said they were not gone to Scotland, but had been traced as far as London, whither their father would go. Jane begged her uncle's assistance, and Lizzy home.

Just then Darcy arrived, and on seeing her pale face he cried, 'Good God! What is the matter?' She told him – he would soon find out, anyway.

He was quiet for some time, thinking, before he left with a polite adieu.

Chapter 46

Chapter 47

Elizabeth soon set off for Longbourn with the Gardiners, who did their best to reassure her. But Elizabeth blamed herself for not telling her family the truth about Wickham.

She was pleased to reach Longbourn the next day; Jane was pale but pleased to see her. Their mother was still in bed, blaming everyone else, and worrying about Lydia's wedding clothes.

Jane showed Lizzy the letter Lydia wrote to Mrs Forster, which began:

'You will laugh when you know where I am gone. I can hardly write for laughing.'

Chapter 47

Chapter 48

All Meryton seemed striving to blacken the man who, but three months before, had been almost an angel of light. He was declared to be in debt to every tradesman in the town.

Mr Bennet returned home to a letter from Mr Collins, telling him, 'The death of your daughter would have been a blessing in comparison to this. Lady Catherine agrees with me that this false step in one daughter will be injurious to the fortunes of all the others.'

The family spent every day in the greatest anxiety.

Chapter 48

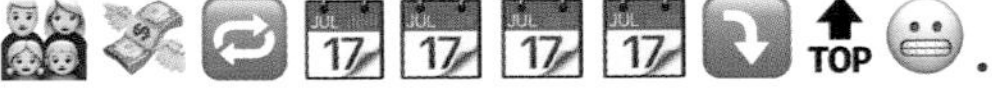

Chapter 49

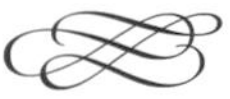

Elizabeth and Jane heard that Mr Bennet had received a letter, and ran to him. He told Elizabeth to read it aloud:

'I have found them both,' Mr Gardiner wrote.

'They are married!' cried Jane.

'They are not married,' Elizabeth read on, 'but if you are willing to give Lydia her equal share of five thousand pounds, I hope it will not be long before they are.'

Mr Bennet expressed his concern at how much Mr Gardiner may have settled on the couple, but knew he must write back and agree the plan. Mrs Bennet squealed with joy when she heard the news.

Chapter 49

Chapter 50

Mrs Bennet was in spirits oppressively high. No sentiment of shame gave a damp to her triumph.

Elizabeth was now heartily sorry that she had made Mr Darcy acquainted with her fears for her sister; she began now to comprehend that he was the man who, in disposition and talents, would most suit her.

Mr Gardiner wrote that Wickham and Lydia would remove to the north, but hoped to be invited to Longbourn first. Mr Bennet refused at first, but in time relented. Elizabeth did not look forward to seeing Wickham.

Chapter 50

Chapter 51

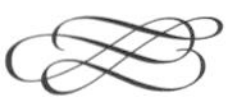

Lydia's wedding day arrived, and then the couple came on to Longbourn. Smiles decked the face of Mrs Bennet; her husband looked grave; her daughters, alarmed, anxious, uneasy.

Lydia and Wickham were in no way embarrassed, but spoke easily of their wedding, and Lydia showed off her ring to everyone.

Lydia let slip that Mr Darcy had attended her wedding, but could not say more.

Elizabeth burned with curiosity, so wrote to her aunt for more information.

Chapter 51

Chapter 52

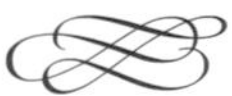

Elizabeth did not have to wait long for an answer. Mrs Gardiner was surprised that Lizzy did not know the truth, so enlightened her: Mr Darcy had found the pair, and expedited a marriage between them. He had battled with Mr Gardiner over who should settle the score financially with Wickham, but Darcy was obstinate.

The letter threw Elizabeth into a flutter of spirits, but Wickham interrupted her thoughts. He tried to engage her in conversation on how Mr Darcy had wronged him, but she made short work of him.

Chapter 52

Chapter 53

Mrs Bennet was sad to say goodbye to Lydia, but distracted by news that Mr Bingley was soon to return to Netherfield to shoot.

Jane told Elizabeth, 'This news does not affect me either with pleasure or pain. Happy shall I be, when his stay at Netherfield is over!'

On the third morning after Mr Bingley's arrival, he called at Longbourn – with Mr Darcy! The latter was very quiet, and Mr Bingley looked pleased but embarrassed. He clearly admired Jane as much as he did a year before.

Chapter 53

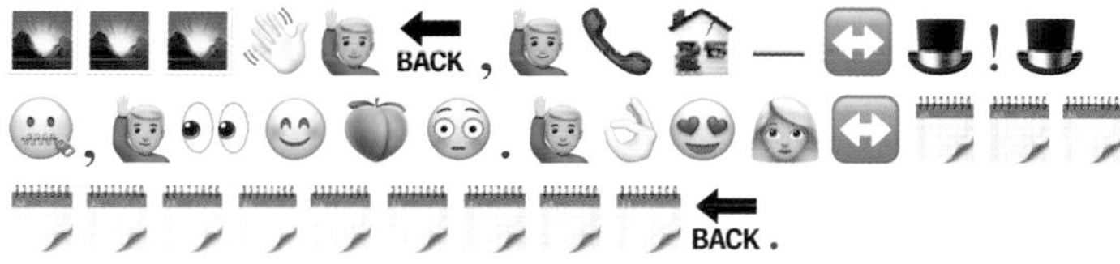

Chapter 54

Mr Darcy's silence astonished and vexed Elizabeth. 'Why, did he come, if only to be silent, grave, and indifferent,' said she. 'Does he fear me, or no longer care for me?'

After they left, Jane was happy the first meeting was over, believing that she and Mr Bingley could soon meet as indifferent acquaintances. Elizabeth tried not to laugh.

The following day, the gentlemen came to dinner. Bingley once again sat by Jane. Elizabeth had little opportunity of speaking to Mr Darcy, and finished the evening frustrated beyond measure.

Chapter 54

Chapter 55

Mr Bingley called so early that none of the ladies were dressed.
When they were all down, Mrs Bennet sat winking at Lizzy and Kitty for some time, before succeeding in removing them.

When Lizzy returned, she found Mr Bingley and Jane standing together over the hearth – finally, they were engaged!

Mrs Bennet was in rapturous delight on hearing the news, and even Mr Bennet had some kind words.
'I have not a doubt of your doing very well together. Your tempers are by no means unlike. You are each of you so complying, that nothing will ever be resolved on; and so generous, that you will always exceed your income.'

Chapter 55

Chapter 56

The Bennets were in the sitting room, when they were surprised by a visit from Lady Catherine de Bourgh. She declined refreshment, not very politely, but asked Elizabeth to walk outside with her.

The reason for her visit, was that she'd heard that her nephew was engaged to Elizabeth. She declared that it must be a scandalous falsehood, but when Elizabeth would not confirm or deny it, Lady Catherine attacked her parents, her sister's elopement, and her lack of wealth.

'Obstinate, headstrong girl! Are the shades of Pemberley to be thus polluted?' Elizabeth told her to leave.

Chapter 56

Chapter 57

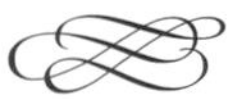

Mr Bennet received a letter from Mr Collins, believing there to be an engagement between Mr Darcy and Lizzy. Mr Bennet laughed, 'He never looked at you in his life!'

He read aloud, 'In spite of all temptation, let me warn you of the evils of a precipitate closure with this gentleman's proposal. Lady Catherine de Bourgh does not look on the marriage with a friendly eye.'

'Are you not diverted? For what do we live, but to make sport for our neighbours, and laugh at them in our turn?'

Lizzy had to pretend to be diverted.

Chapter 57

Chapter 58

Mr Bingley brought Darcy on his next visit and, on a walk, Lizzy and Mr Darcy were finally alone.

'You are too generous to trifle with me,' he said. 'If your feelings are still what they were last April, tell me so at once. My affections and wishes are unchanged, but one word from you will silence me on this subject for ever.'

Lizzy expressed that her sentiments had undergone so material a change, as to make her receive with gratitude his present assurances. The happiness which this reply produced, was such as he had probably never felt before.

Chapter 58

Chapter 59

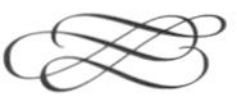

'You are joking, Lizzy. This cannot be! – engaged to Mr Darcy! No, no, you shall not deceive me. I know it to be impossible.' It took some work for Lizzy to convince Jane that she truly loved Mr Darcy.

'Lizzy, what are you doing? Are you out of your senses, to be accepting this man?' It took some work for Lizzy to convince her father that she truly loved Mr Darcy.

'Oh! my sweetest Lizzy! How rich and how great you will be! Three daughters married! Ten thousand a year!' It took very little work for Lizzy to convince her mother that she truly loved Mr Darcy.

Chapter 59

Chapter 60

Elizabeth enjoyed teasing Mr Darcy, but it was time for some letters to be written:

~ Mr Darcy wrote to Lady Catherine, after Lizzy teased him about having the courage to do so. The Collinses came to stay at Lucas Lodge to escape from her wrath.

~ Lizzy wrote a joyful letter to her aunt, inviting them to Pemberley for Christmas.

~ Mr Bennet wrote a triumphant letter to Mr Collins, asking for his congratulations.

~ Miss Bingley wrote a crawling letter to Jane, with the congratulations of a sister... Jane was not fooled, but was still nice.

~ Miss Darcy wrote four sides of her own delight in her new sister.

Chapter 60

-💁‍♀️📝😆✉️➡️👩‍🌾, ✉️🎟️➡️🏰4️⃣🎄🎅
🎁☃️.

-👴📝🏆✉️➡️🤦‍♂️, 🙏🤦‍♂️👏🙌.

-👸📝🌅✉️➡️👩, ↔️👏🙌↗️👭... 👩🚫
🤥➡️🃏, 🍑〰️😌.

-🐭📝📜📜📜📜➡️🐭😁⤵️🆕↗️👭.

Chapter 61

~ Mrs Bennet could not have been prouder to have two daughters so well married.

~ Mr Bennet missed Lizzy a great deal, but enjoyed visiting her at Pemberley.

~ Mr Bingley and Jane remained at Netherfield only a twelvemonth, before they moved near Pemberley.

~ Kitty improved a great deal from time spent in superior society.

~ Lydia wrote to Lizzy asking for money; she sent a little, from time to time.

~ Miss Bingley was civil, so she could continue to visit Pemberley.

~ Georgiana and Lizzy were able to love each other even as well as they hoped.

~ Lady Catherine eventually forgave them.

~ The Gardiners visited often.

~ Elizabeth and Mr Darcy were happy.

- 

- 👴 😞 💢 💁‍♀️ ➕➕, 🍑 😁 ➡️ 👋 💁‍♀️ ⤵️ 🏰.

- 🙋‍♂️ 👩 👇 🏠 📆 📆 📆 📆 📆 📆 📆 📆 📆 📆
📆 📆, 🐝 4️⃣ ➡️ 🏡 ↔️ 🏰.

- 🐱 🔅 🔆 👍 ⬅️ 🕖 🕕 🕚 ⤵️ 🔝 👨‍👩‍👧‍👦 👨‍👩‍👧‍👧 👩‍👩‍👦 👨‍👨‍👦.

- 💃 📝 ➡️ 💁‍♀️ 🙏 💰; 💁‍♀️ 📮 👌 ➡️ 🕓 2️⃣ 🕛.

- 👸 🙂, ➡️ 👸 👋 🏰.

- 💁‍♀️ ➕ 🐭 💪 👩‍❤️‍👩 ↔️ 👍 💁‍♀️ 🐭 🤞.

- 🐉 🕛 🕔 🕐 🕑 ➡️ 🤝 🙇‍♀️ 🙇.
- 👨‍🌾 👩‍🌾 👋 📅 📅 🔄.
- 💁‍♀️ 🎩 😁 😁 💏.

The End